For Goldy

BLOOMSBURY CHILDREN'S BOOKS
Bloomsbury Publishing Inc., part of Bloomsbury Publishing Plc
1385 Broadway, New York, NY 10018

BLOOMSBURY, BLOOMSBURY CHILDREN'S BOOKS, and the Diana logo
are trademarks of Bloomsbury Publishing Plc

First published in Great Britain in July 2022 by Bloomsbury Publishing Plc
Published in the United States of America in February 2023
by Bloomsbury Children's Books

Bloomsbury books may be purchased for business or promotional use. For information on bulk purchases please contact
Macmillan Corporate and Premium Sales Department at specialmarkets@macmillan.com

Library of Congress Cataloging-in-Publication Data
available upon request
ISBN 978-1-5476-1097-6 (hardcover)
ISBN 978-1-5476-1098-3 (e-book) • ISBN 978-1-5476-1099-0 (e-PDF)

Art created digitally using a combination of natural media brushes in Procreate
on an iPad and a Wacom drawing tablet with Adobe Photoshop on an iMac
Typeset in Appareo Medium • Book design by Goldy Broad
Printed and bound in China by Leo Paper Products, Heshan, Guangdong
2 4 6 8 10 9 7 5 3 1

To find out more about our authors and books visit www.bloomsbury.com and sign up for our newsletters.

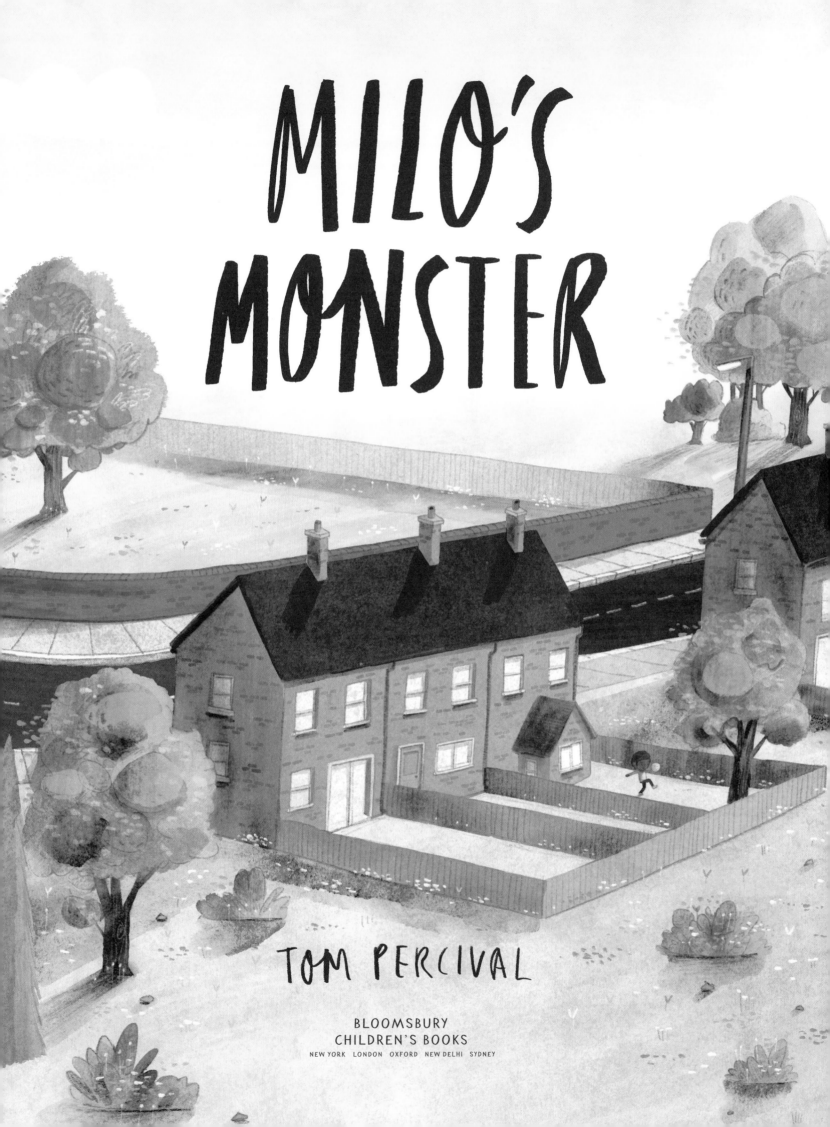

MILO'S MONSTER

TOM PERCIVAL

BLOOMSBURY
CHILDREN'S BOOKS
NEW YORK LONDON OXFORD NEW DELHI SYDNEY

Milo lived in a neat little house
on a neat little street.

He LOVED his home for lots of reasons,
but mainly because . . .

His best friend Jay lived next door!

Milo and Jay shared
the good times,

the bad times,

and everything
in between.

Nothing could beat the feeling
of having a best friend.

Then one day, a new family moved into
the big old house across the street.

Milo watched as a girl ran excitedly around
the yard. She smiled and waved,
and Milo waved back.

Later that afternoon, Milo went to visit Jay,
but he wasn't in. He had gone over to the
big old house **across** the street . . .

without telling Milo.

Jay and the girl were in the yard,
laughing. **Very LOUDLY.**

A funny feeling squirmed
around in Milo's tummy.

"Hi Milo," called Jay. "This is Suzi.
Isn't her yard AMAZING?"

Milo nodded, but the jealous, squirmy feeling had nothing to do with Suzi's massive yard and **everything** to do with how much fun Jay was having . . .

without him!

The next day, Jay was out, AGAIN.

Milo knew exactly
where he would be . . .

And sure enough, he was outside
reading comics with Suzi.

Then Milo had a horrible thought . . .

What if Jay didn't want to be best friends
with him anymore?

The squirmy feeling took over completely.
And as it did, something very strange happened . . .

A GREEN-EYED MONSTER

popped up, right beside him.

"IT'S NOT FAIR!" muttered the monster.
"Jay is YOUR friend, not Suzi's!"

From then on, the green-eyed monster
wouldn't leave him alone!

Whenever he saw Jay and Suzi laughing,
the green-eyed monster said they
were making fun of him.

And whenever he saw them playing . . .

the monster hissed that they were
having more fun without him.

Every time Milo saw Suzi and Jay together,
the green-eyed monster made him feel
TERRIBLE.

So, Milo decided to stop seeing them at all.

If they came to his
house, he pretended
not to be in.

If he saw them at the park,
he would hide.

And if either of them asked what was wrong,
he just said, "Nothing," and turned away.

Day after day, he walked around with only the miserable mutterings of the green-eyed monster for company.

Until one day. . . .

Suzi tapped him on the shoulder.
"Why aren't you and Jay friends anymore?"
she asked. "He really misses you!"

She looked *very* upset.

The monster said it was a trick.
That Suzi was lying.

But Milo shook his head.

It was time to get rid of that pesky monster
once and for all!

Milo shut his eyes tight. He took a deep breath and tried to force the bad feeling away.

The green-eyed monster protested
and muttered mean words—
but its voice became quieter

and quieter,

and quieter,

until at last it was
completely
GONE.

Finally Milo could see the truth.
The green-eyed monster had nearly ruined
EVERYTHING!

Now, he did the only thing that he could.

He said, "I'm sorry."
And he really was.

Soon they were all friends again,
laughing and playing in Suzi's yard—
TOGETHER.

Milo smiled.
Nothing could beat the feeling
of having a best friend . . .

Except having TWO of them!

Dear Reader,

Everyone feels jealous from time to time. It's completely understandable, but that doesn't make it feel any less horrible!

The trouble is that, like Milo, we never know exactly what everyone else is thinking or feeling—so it can be easy to let that pesky green-eyed monster take over!

Here are a few simple tips to help you deal with those jealous feelings.

➤ If you feel like a friendship is getting a bit wobbly, it's always best to explain how you feel to your friend. A good talk always helps to clear the air.
➤ When we're tired, EVERYTHING seems more difficult. So if you're feeling upset with a friend, then take a step back, get a good night's sleep, and talk things through another day.
➤ Talk about how you feel with a trusted adult. They'll be able to help you work through your feelings and offer you advice.

No matter how you're feeling, remember that it always helps to talk about it. Be open, be honest, be YOU!

Love,

TOM

Here's an organization that offers resources if you're interested in learning more: **childmind.org**